This book belongs to

For my brothers Adam and Ben...
and also for Stephen and Chris, who, like the ants,
carry food off Claire's plate and mine!

G.R.

This edition published by Parragon Books Ltd in 2014

Parragon Books Ltd
Chartist House
15–17 Trim Street
Bath BA1 1HA, UK
www.parragon.com

Published by arrangement with Gullane Children's Books

Text and illustrations © Gemma Raynor 2013

ISBN 978-1-4723-4598-1

Printed in China

Anthony and the Ants

Gemma Raynor

PaRRagon

Bath · New York · Cologne · Melbourne · Delhi
Hong Kong · Shenzhen · Singapore · Amsterdam

This is what happened at **breakfast** today -

Anthony's food walked away!

And sadly that was not the end of that...

At **lunch**

At **dinner**

his food leapt from the table.

it dashed down the hall.

"Oh what could it be?" poor Anthony cried...

Ants!

Cheeky...

sneaky,

greedy

little

ants!

Every time Anthony opened his mouth...

his food had been **carried away!**

Anthony could take no more...

Snatching an apple, he ran for the door.

Off he sped and up he flew...

far away to somewhere new.

"I JUST WANT TO EAT
THIS APPLE IN PEACE.

Perfect!"

"I agree..."

said a
BIG HUNGRY BEAR!
"A PERFECT time
for you to drop by!"

And he opened his mouth...

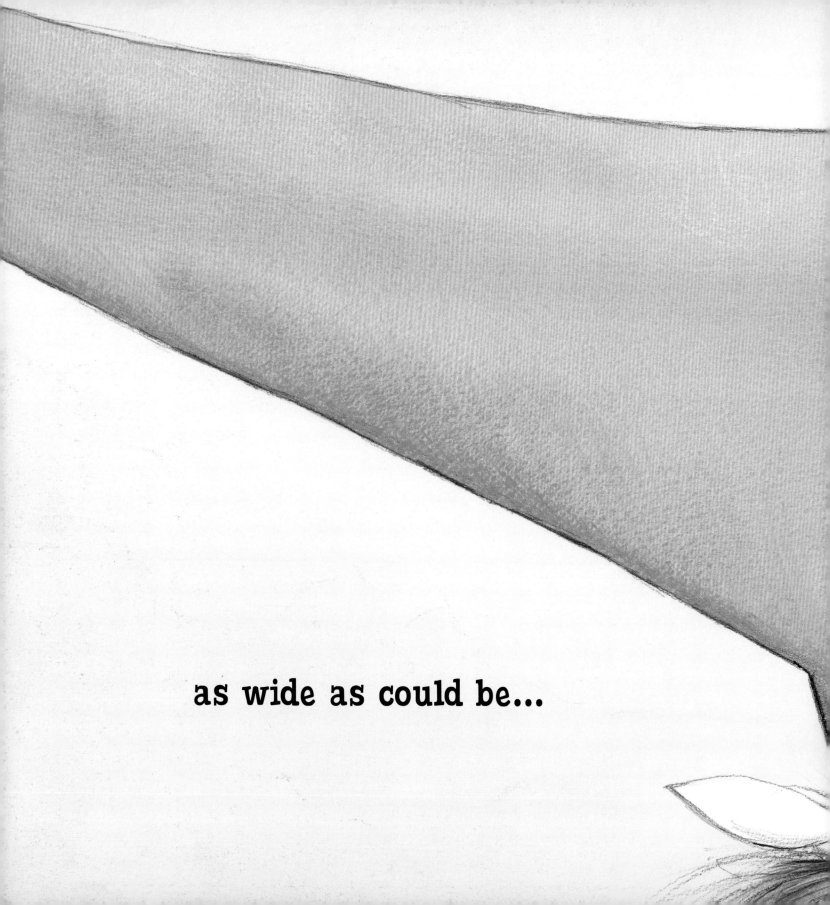

as wide as could be...

then all of a sudden his breakfast was

carried away!

By ants of course,
small, brave and strong!

Now will everyone FINALLY get along?

Yes! For it seems those ants have learned something too...

Sharing really is best!